Fun with numbers

Ray Gibson

Illustrated by Amanda Barlow

Edited by Fiona Watt

Series editor : Jenny Tyler

Contents

Getting started

This book is full of different activities, like the one below, which involve counting, adding, taking away or sharing. Some of the pages ask you to cut paper shapes to help you to count. You don't need to worry about how neat they are.

Going shopping

How many things are in this basket?

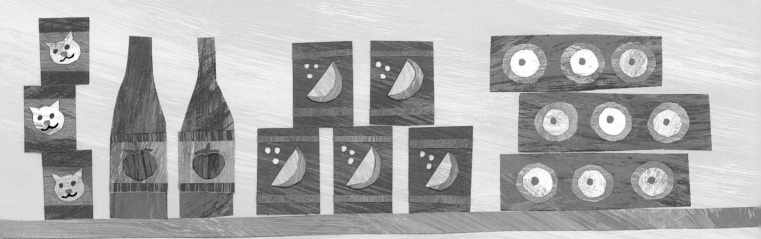

Cut pictures of any kind of food from a magazine or newspaper.

Put the pictures in this empty basket so that both baskets contain the same number of things.

3

Sailing boats

How many boats
are there
altogether?

How many boats
have **2** sails?

Cut sails from
paper and put
them on the boats
so that each one
has **2** sails.

How many sails are
there now?

Spiders' Legs

How many spiders
are there
altogether?

How many legs
does each spider
have?

Which spider has
the most legs?

Cut some pieces
of yarn for legs.
Put them on the
spider so that each
one has **8** legs.

7

Busy cranes

How many boxes is each crane lifting?
How many boxes are the cranes
lifting altogether?

Cut some boxes from paper.
Add 1 box to each crane.
How many boxes are there
altogether now?

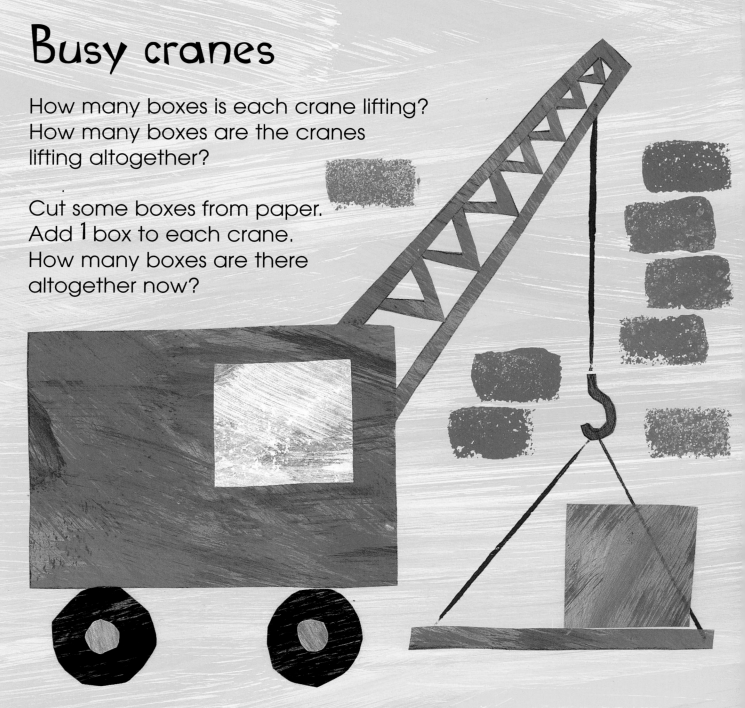

Add another box to each crane.
How many boxes are the cranes lifting now?

Planes

How many planes can you see?

Cut clouds from paper and cover 3 planes. How many planes can you see now?

Cover **2** more planes
with paper clouds.
How many planes
are left?

Shy monkeys

How many monkeys are in the tree?

Cut big leaves from paper and put them over the small monkeys to hide them.

How many monkeys are left?

Hold up 1 finger for each monkey that is left.

One monkey goes looking for food. Put 1 finger down. How many monkeys are left now?

Builders' trucks

Cut out some bricks from paper. Put 3 bricks on the back of each truck.

Draw a circle with your finger around each group of 3 bricks.

How many groups of 3 are there?

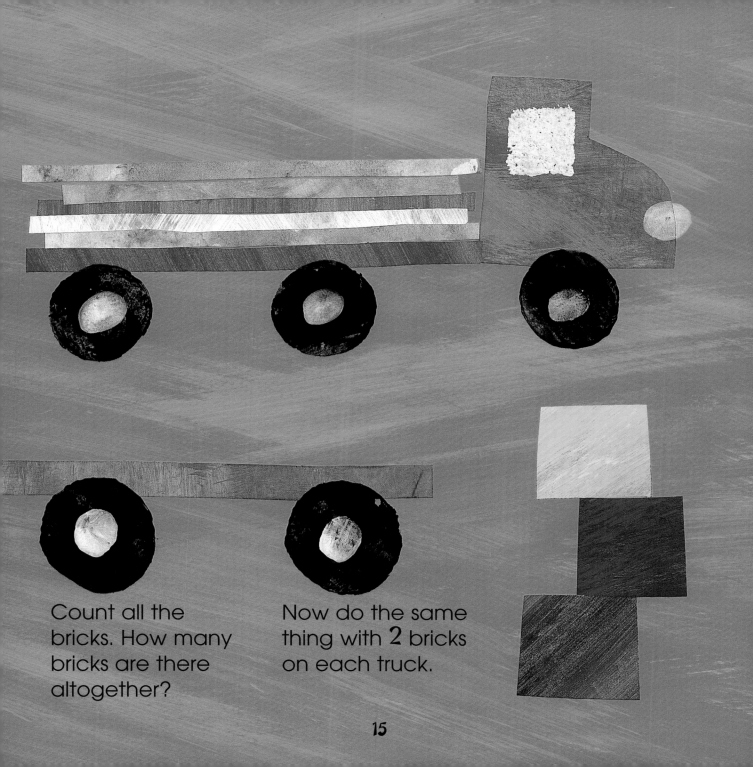

Count all the bricks. How many bricks are there altogether?

Now do the same thing with 2 bricks on each truck.

Greedy parrots

Use pieces of pasta as treats for the parrots.

Guess how many treats you will need, for each parrot to have 1 treat.
Give each parrot 1 treat to see if you were correct.

Give each parrot 2 treats.
How many treats are there altogether?

Give each parrot 3 treats.
How many are there now?

Roly-poly puppies

Cut 2 plastic straws into 12 pieces to make pretend bones.

Share the bones between the puppies until they have all been used up.

Share all the bones between 2 puppies. How many bones does each one have?

Try sharing all the bones between 3 puppies. How many does each one have now?

Four fat bears

Squeeze small
pieces of kitchen
foil to make **10** little
fish shapes.

Give each bear
2 fish.
How many fish are
left over?

How many bears
can have 3 fish
each?
How many fish are
left over?

How many bears
can have 4 fish
each?

Jumping frogs

Make a frog like this.

Fold some paper.

Make two snips.

Fold back the paper between the snips.

Draw on a face and some front legs.

Put your frog on the big lily pad.

Make your frog jump on each pink lily until it gets to the reeds. How many jumps does it make?

How many jumps
does your frog make
if it goes on the
yellow lilies instead?

23

Spotted giraffes

Count the spots on the big giraffe. Then count the spots on the baby giraffe. Which has more spots?

Cut **5** spots from paper and put them on the baby. Which giraffe has more spots now? Which has the least spots?

Add a different
number of spots
to the baby.
Which has more
spots, now?

Party cakes

How many plates have **6** cakes on them?

Cut out shapes from paper to make cakes. Put them on the plates so that all the plates have **6** cakes.

How many cakes did you add to the white plate to make **6**?
How many did you add to the blue plate?
How many did you add to the yellow plate?

Something fishy

Cut small shapes from paper, about the size of the spots on the fish.

Cover each spot on the orange fish below, with a paper shape. How many shapes did you need?

Cover the spots on the other fish. How many shapes did you need each time?

Look at the patterns of the spots on the fish.

Make a pattern with 4 paper shapes on the fish with no spots.

29

Busy bees

Draw **3** small bees and cut them out. Put **1** on each big flower.
Cut out **9** small squares
Draw pink spots on **3** squares, blue spots on **3** and purple spots on **3**.

Put the squares into a bag, then pull one out. If it's pink, move the bee on the pink flower along one.
If it's purple, move the bee on the purple flower, and so on.

Put the square back into the bag. Have lots more turns.

Which bee reaches the beehive first?
Which is second?
Which bee came third?

31

How many spots?

Count the spots in each picture.

Fold some kitchen foil around a piece of cardboard, for a mirror. Stand it along the straight edge of each picture so you can see its other half. Count again. How many spots does each creature have now?